¡Muu, Moo!

Rimas de animales
Animal Nursery Rhymes

Selected by Alma Flor Ada and F. Isabel Campoy
English versions by Rosalma Zubizarreta
Illustrated by Viví Escrivá

rayo

An Imprint of HarperCollinsPublishers

Rayo is an imprint of HarperCollins Publishers.

¡Muu, Moo!
Spanish compilation copyright © 2010 by Alma Flor Ada and F. Isabel Campoy
English adaptations copyright © 2010 by Rosalma Zubizarreta
Illustrations copyright © 2010 by Viví Escrivá
Manufactured in China.
Library of Congress Cataloging-in-Publication Data is available.
ISBN 978-0-06-134613-2 (trade bdg.)—ISBN 978-0-06-134614-9 (lib. bdg.)
Typography by Matt Adamec
10 11 12 13 14 SCP 10 9 8 7 6 5 4 3 2 1
❖
First Edition

To Diego García-Campoy IV and Collette Zubizarreta.
May our cultural heritage live happily in your hearts.
And to the cows that brightened our childhoods.
—F.I.C. and A.F.A.

OUR SINCERE GRATITUDE:

To Rosemary Brosnan, for bridging New York and San Francisco with acts of friendship and wisdom.

To Suni Paz, *hermana* in the love of poetry and music.

To Camila Zubizaretta, whose humor created the title for this book.

AUTHORS' NOTE:

Oral folklore in Spanish is rich in rhymes. Some rhymes tell a story, such as *Patito, patito* and *El gallo Espolón;* others have a surprising and humorous ending, such as *El gato y el ratón* and *Las once y media serían.* Still others simply capture a moment in time, as does *Una paloma blanca.*

For this book, we have chosen verses with an animal theme. Along the way, we reviewed numerous anthologies, including ones by María Elena Walsh and Elsa Isabel Bornemann from Argentina; *Niños y alas* from the University of Puerto Rico; the series *Así cantan y juegan . . .* published by CONAFE in Mexico; and the anthologies of Carmen Bravo-Villasante, Arturo Medina, and Ana Pelegrín from Spain. From the hundreds of rhymes we reviewed, we chose those we remember with joy from our own childhoods and ones that the numerous children with whom we have worked—from Mexico, Puerto Rico, Cuba, the Dominican Republic, and Central America—have loved the most.

It has been a joy to complement the traditional selections with some new verses of our own creation. This book is an invitation to keep folklore alive by remembering, collecting, and sharing traditional rhymes, as well as by allowing our cherished traditions to inspire our contemporary work today.

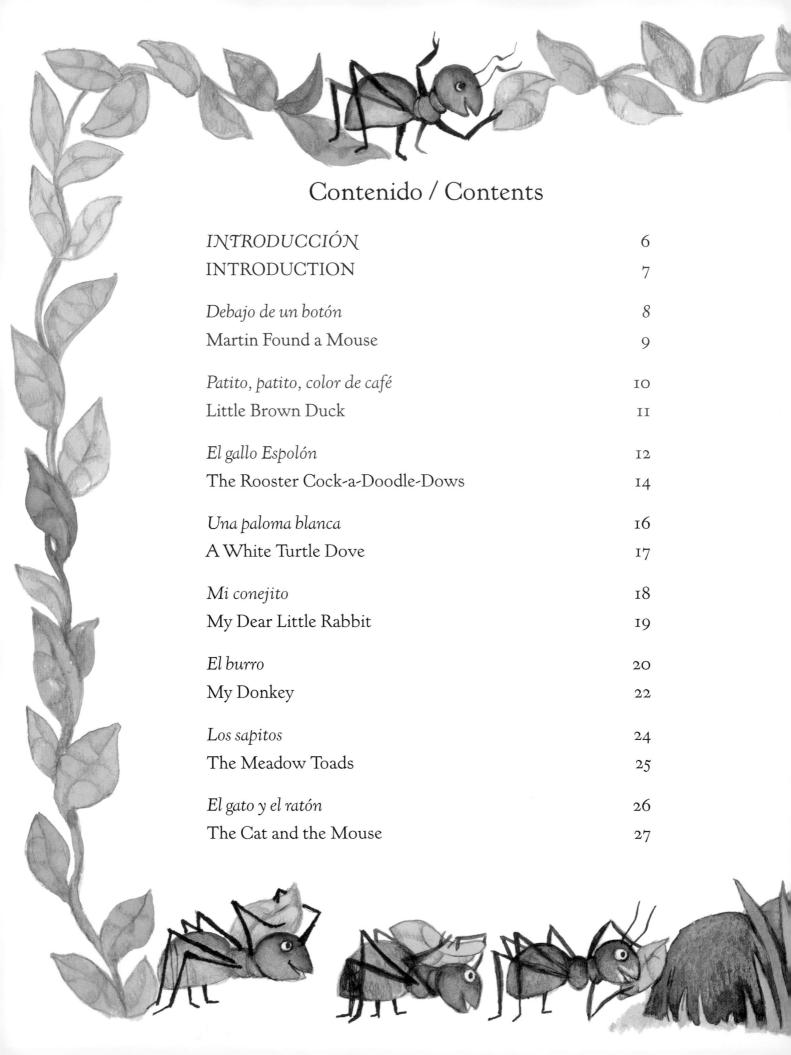

Contenido / Contents

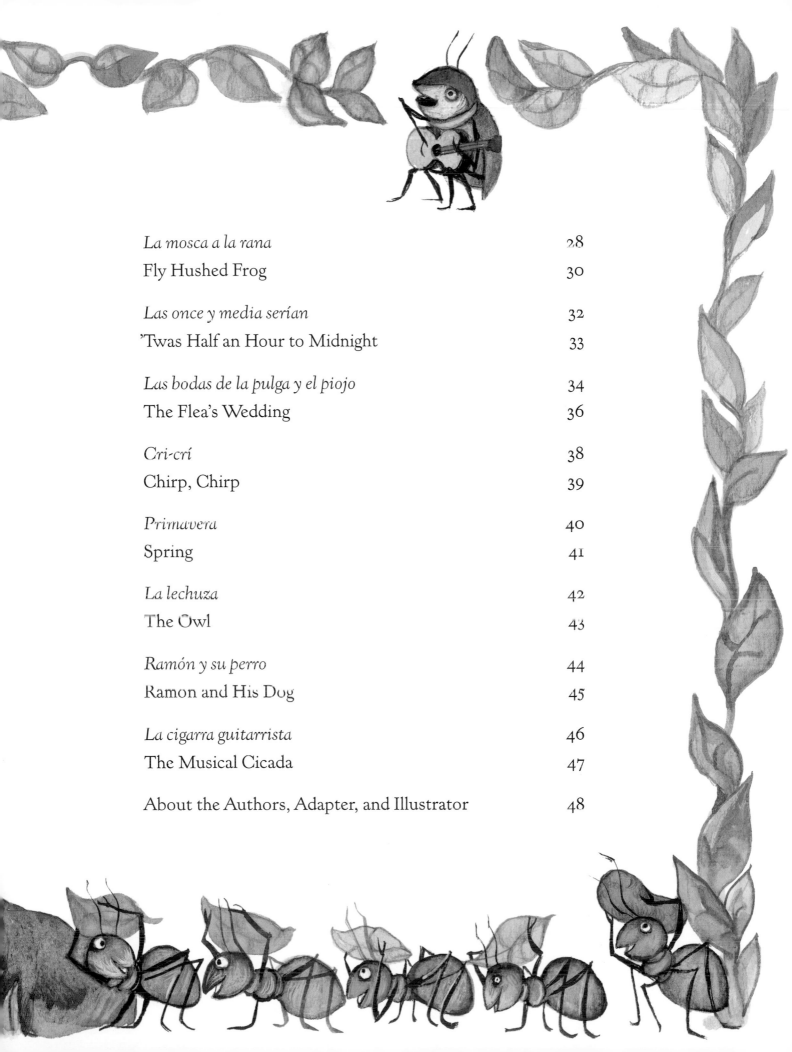

Introducción

Ya sea siguiendo el vuelo de los pájaros o el caminar de una hormiga, acariciando a un gato, jugando con un perro o descubriendo los animales de las granjas, la selva o el mar, los animales ocupan un lugar preferencial en la rica imaginación infantil.

Las palabras, a su vez, son motivo de fascinación para los niños. En el extraordinario proceso de adquirir el idioma, se recrean con rimas y aliteraciones, aprendiendo a jugar con los sonidos. Por eso el folklore infantil deja un recuerdo tan profundo.

Los niños de habla inglesa encontrarán en este libro rimas llenas de ternura y humor sobre sus amigos los animales. No han sido traducidas, sino recreadas poéticamente para así mantener el encanto del original. Para los niños latinos este libro representa un puente entre la infancia de sus antepasados y su propia infancia. Para tener buenos frutos es necesario tener buenas raíces. Este libro se sustenta en esas raíces amplias de una historia que se expande, ramifica y desarrolla con características únicas en cada uno de los veinte países donde se habla español; una historia que vuelve a reunirse aquí, en los Estados Unidos.

Para reconocer la fuerza vibrante de la cultura latina ofrecemos algunas de las rimas más apreciadas por los niños en España y América Latina, así como algunas originales creadas en los Estados Unidos. Y porque los latinos sabemos el valor de ser bilingües, esta antología también lo es. Invitamos a los padres y maestros a recordar su propia infancia para crear una comunicación eficaz entre el ayer y el mañana. Sigamos haciendo camino al andar.

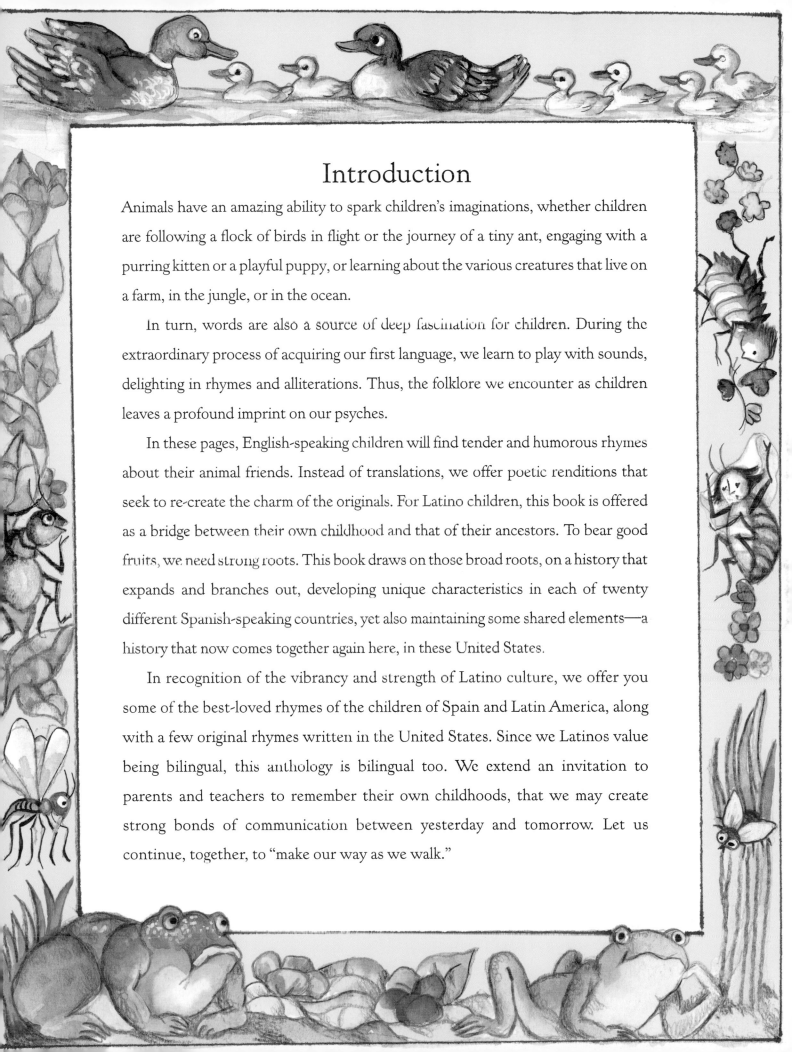

Introduction

Animals have an amazing ability to spark children's imaginations, whether children are following a flock of birds in flight or the journey of a tiny ant, engaging with a purring kitten or a playful puppy, or learning about the various creatures that live on a farm, in the jungle, or in the ocean.

In turn, words are also a source of deep fascination for children. During the extraordinary process of acquiring our first language, we learn to play with sounds, delighting in rhymes and alliterations. Thus, the folklore we encounter as children leaves a profound imprint on our psyches.

In these pages, English-speaking children will find tender and humorous rhymes about their animal friends. Instead of translations, we offer poetic renditions that seek to re-create the charm of the originals. For Latino children, this book is offered as a bridge between their own childhood and that of their ancestors. To bear good fruits, we need strong roots. This book draws on those broad roots, on a history that expands and branches out, developing unique characteristics in each of twenty different Spanish-speaking countries, yet also maintaining some shared elements—a history that now comes together again here, in these United States.

In recognition of the vibrancy and strength of Latino culture, we offer you some of the best-loved rhymes of the children of Spain and Latin America, along with a few original rhymes written in the United States. Since we Latinos value being bilingual, this anthology is bilingual too. We extend an invitation to parents and teachers to remember their own childhoods, that we may create strong bonds of communication between yesterday and tomorrow. Let us continue, together, to "make our way as we walk."

Debajo de un botón

TRADICIONAL

Debajo de un botón, ton ton,
que encontró Martín, tin, tin
había un ratón, ton, ton,
¡ay, que chiquitín, tin, tin!

¡Ay, que chiquitín, tin, tin,
era el ratón, ton, ton,
que encontró Martín, tin, tin,
debajo de un botón, ton, ton!

Martin Found a Mouse

Martin found a mouse, mouse, mouse,
'neath a button on the floor, floor, floor,
in a tiny house, house, house,
with a tiny door, door, door.

In that tiny house, house, house,
with the tiny door, door, door,
Martin found a mouse, mouse, mouse,
'neath a button on the floor, floor, floor.

Patito, patito, color de café
Tradicional adaptado

—Patito, patito,
color de café,
¿por qué estás tan triste?
quisiera saber.

—Mi pata perdí.
Del nido se fue.
Por eso estoy triste
y triste estaré.

—Patito, patito,
color de café,
hoy ya no estás triste,
dime por qué.

—No lejos de aquí
mi pata encontré
con ocho patitos
color de café.

—Yo ya no estoy triste
y no lo estaré.
Ahora estoy contento
y feliz seré.

Little Brown Duck

Oh, little brown duck,
you look so full of woe.
Why are you so sad?
I'd really like to know.

I've lost my duckie wife,
I've been searching all around.
That's why I feel so sad.
She is nowhere to be found.

Oh, little brown duck,
you no longer look so sad!
Today you look quite happy!
Why are you so glad?

Not too far from here,
I found my duckie wife,
with eight new little babies,
brown ducklings full of life!

So I'm no longer sad,
and I'm no longer blue.
I've never felt so happy,
and my wife is happy too!

El gallo Espolón

TRADICIONAL ADAPTADO

Este es el gallo Espolón
verás lo que le pasó.

Esta es la casa de Antón
y éste es Ric-Ric el ratón
que comía del montón
de maíz que en el granero
tenía en la casa Antón.
Este es el gato Ron-Ron
que perseguía al ratón
que comía del montón
de maíz que en el granero
tenía en la casa Antón.
Este es el perro Botón
que le ladraba a Ron-Ron
que perseguía al ratón
que comía del montón
de maíz que en el granero
tenía en la casa Antón.

Este es el gallo Espolón
que asustó al perro Botón
que le ladraba a Ron-Ron
que perseguía al ratón
que comía del montón
de maíz que en el granero
tenía en la casa Antón.
Y este es el mozo Simón
que calló al gallo Espolón
que asustó al perro Botón
que le ladraba a Ron-Ron
que perseguía al ratón
que comía del montón
de maíz que en el granero
tenía en la casa Antón.

The Rooster Cock-a-Doodle-Dows

This is the story of a rooster named Cock-a-Doodle-Dows,
And as you'll see, it all started with a very tiny mouse. . . .

This is Anthony's house
And this is Ric-Ric the mouse,
Who feasted on the mountain of corn
Stored inside the great big barn
Standing behind Anthony's house.
This is the cat Meow-Meows,
Who loved to chase Ric-Ric the mouse,
Who feasted on the mountain of corn
Stored inside the great big barn
Standing behind Anthony's house.

This is the dog Bow-Wows,

Who barked at the cat Meow-Meows,

Who loved to chase Ric-Ric the mouse,

Who feasted on the mountain of corn

Stored inside the great big barn

Standing behind Anthony's house.

This is the rooster Cock-a-Doodle-Dows,

Who frightened the dog Bow-Wows,

Who barked at the cat Meow-Meows,

Who loved to chase Ric-Ric the mouse,

Who feasted on the mountain of corn

Stored inside the great big barn

Standing behind Anthony's house.

And this is the young man Simon Strauss,

Who hushed the rooster Cock-a-Doodle Dows,

Who frightened the dog Bow-Wows,

Who barked at the cat Meow-Meows,

Who loved to chase Ric-Ric the mouse,

Who feasted on the mountain of corn

Stored inside the great big barn

Standing behind Anthony's house.

Una paloma blanca
TRADICIONAL ADAPTADO

Una paloma blanca

desde el cielo bajó

en el pico una rama,

en la rama una flor.

En la flor una niña

en su mano un limón,

son sus ojos más lindos

que los rayos del sol.

A White Turtle Dove

A white turtle dove
flew down from above.
In her beak was a branch;
on the branch was a flower;
on the flower was a girl
who held a lemon in her hand
and whose eyes shone more brightly
than the rays of the sun!

Mi conejito
TRADICIONAL

Salta mi conejito

para tus orejitas

come tu zacatito,

mi conejito, conejo mío.

Tristes están los campos

desde que tú te fuiste.

Pero yo estoy contenta

porque te canto, mi conejito.

My Dear Little Rabbit

Hop, little rabbit,
perk up your ears,
nibble on sweet grass,
little rabbit, dear.

The fields are sad and lonely,
ever since you've been gone,
and yet I feel so happy
singing you my song.

El burro

TRADICIONAL

A mi burro, a mi burro
le duele la cabeza,
el médico le ha puesto
una corbata negra.

A mi burro, a mi burro
le duele la garganta,
el médico le ha puesto
una corbata blanca.

A mi burro, a mi burro
le duelen las orejas,
el médico le ha puesto
una gorrita negra.

A mi burro, a mi burro
le duele el corazón,
el médico le ha dado
jarabe de limón.

A mi burro, a mi burro
ya no le duele nada,
el médico le ha dado
jarabe de manzana.

My Donkey

My donkey told me today
his head is hurting, oh my!
The doctor said that he should
put on a long black tie.

My donkey told me today
his throat is hurting, oh my!
The doctor said that he should
put on a long white tie.

My donkey told me today
his ears are hurting, oh no!
The doctor said that he should
wear a black hat just so.

My donkey told me today
his heart is hurting, he thinks.
The doctor decided to give him
some lemon syrup to drink.

My donkey told me today
he no longer hurts at all!
The doctor decided to give him
some apple syrup this fall.

Los sapitos

TRADICIONAL

Los sapos de la laguna

huyen de la tempestad;

los chiquitos dicen: tunga,

y los grandes: tungairá.

¡Sapito que tunga y tunga,

sapito que tungairá!

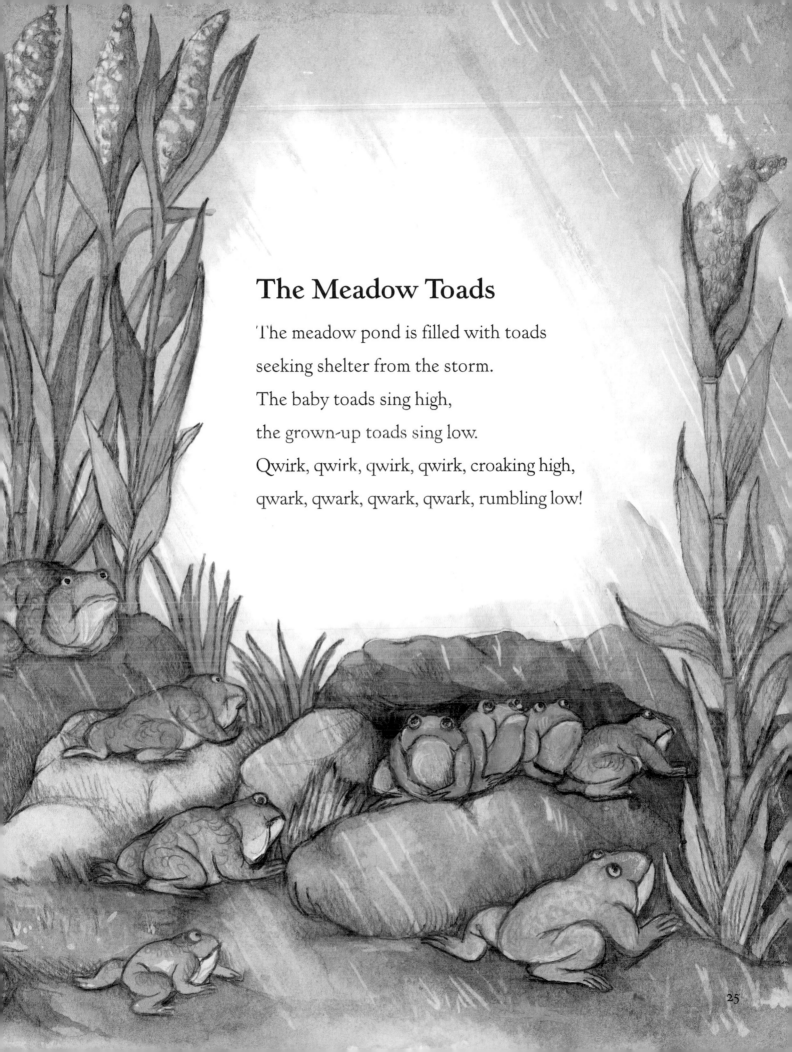

The Meadow Toads

The meadow pond is filled with toads
seeking shelter from the storm.
The baby toads sing high,
the grown-up toads sing low.
Qwirk, qwirk, qwirk, qwirk, croaking high,
qwark, qwark, qwark, qwark, rumbling low!

El gato y el ratón
<small>Tradicional</small>

Estaba una vez un gato
comiéndose una sardina
y un ratón lo contemplaba
asomándose a una esquina.

De repente, al pobre gato,
se le atraganta una espina.
Y el ratón al ver el caso
hacia el gato se encamina.

Y con unos alicates,
¡logra sacarle la espina!

The Cat and the Mouse

Once there was a great big cat
Feasting on a tasty fish
While a tiny mouse looked on
Peeking from behind a dish.

All of a sudden the great big cat
Started choking on a bone.
Seeing this, the tiny mouse
Ran straight up to the cat, all alone . . .

And with a big huge pair of pliers
Managed to pry out the bone!

La mosca a la rana

Tradicional adaptado

Estaba la rana
sentada debajo del agua.
Cuando la rana se puso a cantar
vino la mosca y la hizo callar.

La mosca a la rana
que estaba cantando debajo del agua.
Cuando la mosca se puso a cantar
vino el mosquito y la hizo callar.

El mosquito a la mosca,
la mosca a la rana
que estaba cantando debajo del agua.
Cuando el mosquito se puso a cantar
vino el sapo y lo hizo callar.

El sapo al mosquito,
el mosquito a la mosca,
la mosca a la rana
que estaba cantando debajo del agua.
Cuando el sapo se puso a cantar
vino la gata y lo hizo callar.

La gata al sapo,
el sapo al mosquito,
el mosquito a la mosca,
la mosca a la rana que estaba cantando
debajo del agua.
Cuando la gata se puso a cantar
vine yo y la hice callar.

Fly Hushed Frog

On the bottom of the pond,
Froggy decided to sing a song.
All of a sudden, Fly came along
And made poor Froggy hush her song.

Fly hushed Frog,
Who sang while she sat at the bottom of the pond.
When Fly decided it was her turn to sing,
Along came 'Skeeter to hush her song.

'Skeeter hushed Fly,
Fly hushed Frog,
Who sang while she sat at the bottom of the pond.
When 'Skeeter decided it was her turn to sing,
Along came Toad to hush her song.

Toad hushed 'Skeeter,

'Skeeter hushed Fly,

Fly hushed Frog,

Who sang while she sat at the bottom of the pond.

When Toad decided it was her turn to sing,

Along came Cat to hush her song.

Cat hushed Toad,

Toad hushed 'Skeeter,

'Skeeter hushed Fly,

Fly hushed Frog,

Who sang while she sat at the bottom of the pond.

When Cat decided it was her turn to sing,

I came along to hush her song!

31

Las once y media serían

Las once y media serían

cuando sentí ruido en casa.

Bajo corriendo y ¡qué veo!

que se paseaba una araña.

Lleno de furia y valor

saco mi luciente espada.

Y al primer tajo que doy

¡cae al suelo desmayada!

¡Qué cosa tan prodigiosa!

¿Vuelvo otra vez a contarla?

'Twas Half an Hour to Midnight

'Twas half an hour to midnight
when I heard a frightening sound.
I rushed downstairs to find
a spider was running around!

Filled with fury and courage,
I drew my shining sword.
Just one thrust, and the spider
fainted and fell to the floor.

'Twas quite an amazing feat, my friend!
Shall I tell you the story again?

Las bodas de la pulga y el piojo

La pulga y el piojo se van a casar,
si no se han casado es por falta de pan.

Responde la hormiga desde su hormigal:
—Que se hagan las bodas, yo les daré el pan.

—¡Albricias, albricias, ya el pan lo tenemos!
Pero ahora quien cante, ¿dónde lo hallaremos?

Dice la paloma desde el palomar:
—Que se hagan las bodas, que yo iré a cantar.

—¡Albricias, albricias, quien cante tenemos!
Pero ahora quien baile, ¿dónde lo hallaremos?

Responde una mona desde el cocotal:
—Que se hagan las bodas, que yo iré a bailar.

—¡Albricias, albricias, quien baile tenemos!
Pero ahora madrina, ¿dónde la hallaremos?

Responde la gata desde la cocina:
—Que se hagan las bodas, yo seré madrina.

—¡Albricias, albricias, madrina tenemos!
Pero ahora padrino, ¿dónde lo hallaremos?

Responde un ratón, de su ratonal:
—Si amarran la gata, yo iré a apadrinar.

Y estando las bodas en todo esplendor,
saltó la madrina y se comió al ratón.

¡Ay, que tontería lo que sucedió!
Se soltó la gata, la boda acabó.

The Flea's Wedding

The flea and the louse are planning to wed
As soon as they plan how their guests can all be fed.

The ant hears the news, and calls out from her bed:
"Let the wedding feast begin, I will bring the bread."

"It's time to celebrate! We have bread, and we thank you!
But who will come and sing for us? Oh, what shall we do?"

A dove hears the news and sends word along:
"Let the wedding feast begin, I will bring a song."

"It's time to celebrate! We have a song, and we thank you!
But who will come and dance for us? Oh, what shall we do?"

A monkey hears the news, and she decides at once:
"Let the wedding feast begin, I will come and dance."

"It's time to celebrate! We have a dancer, and we thank you!
But who will be our maid of honor? Oh, what shall we do?"

A cat hears the news, and looks up from her dinner:
"Let the wedding feast begin, I'll be the maid of honor."

"It's time to celebrate! We have a maid of honor, and we thank you!
But who will be our best man? Oh, what shall we do?"

A mouse hears the news and says, "I will do what I can.
If you tie up the cat, I will be your best man."

Yet shortly after the wedding vows,
The cat got loose and gobbled up the mouse!

Oh, what a foolish happening!
Pounce went the cat, and the feast had to end.

Cri-crí

Alma Flor Ada

Verde cri-crí
del grillo alegre saltarín.
Sobre la rama,
bajo la hoja,
junto a la yerba,
sobre la flor.

Cri-crí saltando,
cri-crí llamando,
cri-crí cantando,
se pasa el día,
cri-cri-cri-cando.

Chirp, Chirp

ALMA FLOR ADA

Perky little cricket
With a bright chirp, chirp,
Resting on a branch,
Hiding beneath a leaf,
Playing in the grass,
Perched on a flower.

With a chirp, chirp leap,
And a chirp, chirp call,
And a chirp, chirp song,
Perky little cricket chirps
All day long.

Primavera

Alma Flor Ada

En el prado el caracol
saca los cuernos al sol.
Como premio, el girasol
le da un beso al caracol.

La abejita presurosa
saluda a la flor preciosa.
¡Qué promesa, la primera
mañana de primavera!

Spring

ALMA FLOR ADA

A tiny snail is winding along,

Stretching his feelers toward the sun.

When she sees the snail in bliss,

A sunflower leans over to give him a kiss.

A busy bee joins in the play,

Buzzing over to say, "Good day!"

Oh, what delights a day can bring

On this very first morning of Spring!

La lechuza

F. Isabel Campoy

U, u, u,

oigo en la noche un revuelo.

U, u, u,

una lechuza en su vuelo.

U, u, u,

me da mucho miedo.

U, u, u,

—Mamá, ¡enciende la luz!

The Owl

F. ISABEL CAMPOY

Boo, hoo, hoo,

In the night I hear a cry

Boo, hoo, hoo,

It's an owl, fluttering by

Boo, hoo, hoo,

The eerie sound gives me a fright!

Boo, hoo, hoo—

Mom! Please turn on the light!

43

Ramón y su perro

F. Isabel Campoy

Ramón remaba su barca
por el río Paraná.
Mientras él movía los remos,
a su lado iba cantando
su perrito: Tralalá.
Tralalá, tralalá
por el río Paraná.

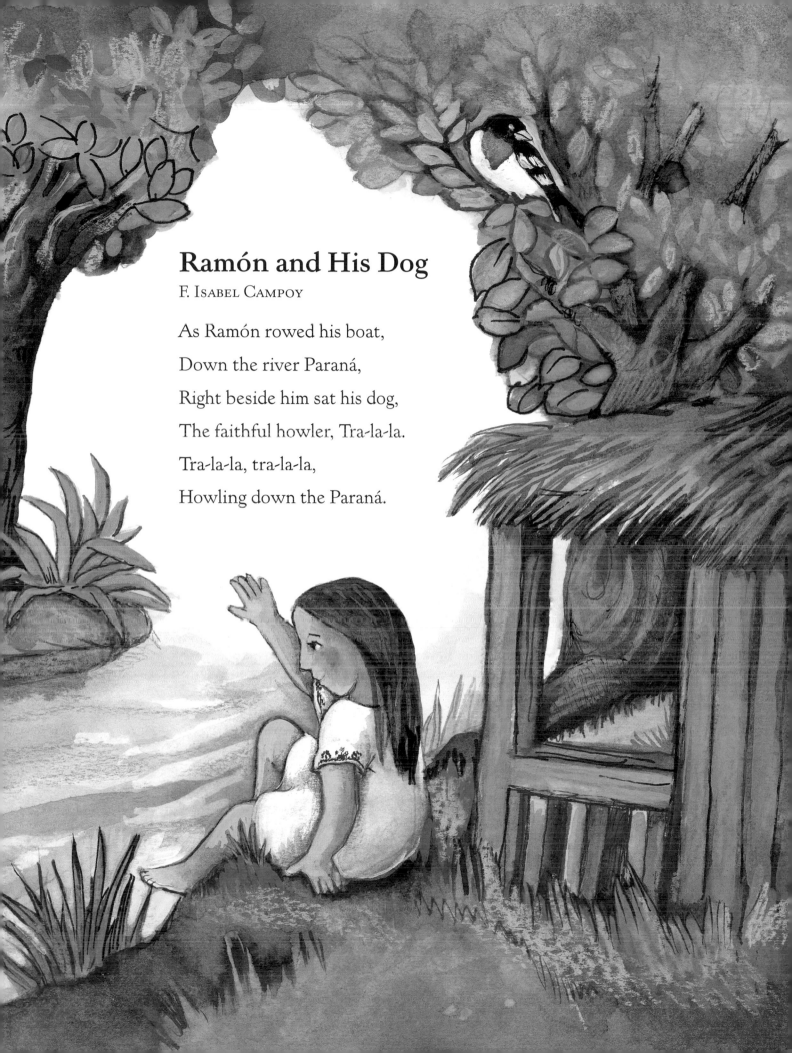

Ramón and His Dog

F. Isabel Campoy

As Ramón rowed his boat,
Down the river Paraná,
Right beside him sat his dog,
The faithful howler, Tra-la-la.
Tra-la-la, tra-la-la,
Howling down the Paraná.

La cigarra guitarrista

NUEVA VERSIÓN DE UNA VIEJA FÁBULA
ALMA FLOR ADA

Cuando el sol sale y se asoma,
Celestina, la cigarra,
subidita en una rama,
canta y toca la guitarra.

Cargando hojitas y migas,
se afana Juana, la hormiga,
y goza escuchando el canto
de la cigarrita amiga.

Y cuando llegue el invierno,
la hormiguita y la cigarra
comerán migas y hojas
y tocarán la guitarra.

The Musical Cicada

A NEW VERSION OF AN OLD FABLE
BY ALMA FLOR ADA

As the sun comes out to see
What this lovely new day brings,
Celestina the cicada
Strums her guitar while she sings.

Juana the ant is hard at work
Gathering leaves and crumbs,
Listening meanwhile to the sounds
Her friend is making as she strums.

When cold wintertime arrives,
Both ant and cicada will then
Savor the taste of crumbs and leaves
And make joyful music again!

About the Authors

Alma Flor Ada has devoted her life to promoting cross-cultural understanding and peace through children's literature as well as enabling children to learn about their cultural heritage. "The words of nursery rhymes and songs gave both wings and roots to my soul," she declares, "and for that reason I enjoy finding ways to continue sharing these treasures with children." Alma Flor Ada delights in studying, collecting, and anthologizing folklore as well as retelling folktales. Director of the Center for Multicultural Literature for Children and Young Adults at the University of San Francisco, Alma Flor Ada is the recipient of numerous academic and literary awards. Among them are the American Library Association's Pura Belpré Award, the Christopher Award, Aesop's Accolade, Parents' Choice Honors, Latina Writers Award, José Martí World Awards, and the Marta Salotti Gold Medal.

F. Isabel Campoy, poet, playwright, storyteller, and researcher of Hispanic culture, has devoted her life to the world of words. As a linguist, she has published numerous articles and textbooks for and about English-language learners and Spanish-language learners. She is the co-author of *Puertas al sol / Gateways to the Sun*, a collection of children's books about art, theater, poetry, biography, and culture in the Hispanic world. Her book *Authors in the Classroom*, co-authored with Alma Flor Ada, showcases her work with teachers, parents, and children, inspiring them to use their life experiences as the basis for authoring their own books. She is the recipient of several distinguished awards for her work, which also includes *Tales Our Abuelitas Told* and *¡Pío Peep!* Affirming the value of folklore, she states, "Words set to music convey the pleasure of rhythm, much like a beating heart!"

About the Adapter

Rosalma Zubizarreta was born in Lima, Peru, and came to the United States as a child. She learned the art of translation at home and particularly appreciates the challenge of working with poetry and song. In addition to translating, editing, and writing, she also enjoys her practice as a consultant in organization development. "Communication is the common thread in the different kinds of work that I do. When I am facilitating a group, I want to help people understand one another better; when I am translating a story or a poem, I want to make it possible for readers to enjoy the grace and spirit of the author's original work."

About the Illustrator

Viví Escrivá is a celebrated illustrator from Spain whose work is also popular in the United States and Europe. *¡Muu, Moo!* is one of the many books on which she has collaborated with Alma Flor Ada and F. Isabel Campoy. Others include *¡Pío Peep!* and *Merry Navidad!* In addition to illustrating books, Viví Escrivá has crafted imaginative large marionettes. She is from a family of illustrators and lives in Madrid, Spain.